Mike THE KNIGHT

Meet Mike!

SIMON AND SCHUSTER
First published in Great Britain in 2012 by Simon and Schuster UK Ltd
1st Floor, 222 Gray's Inn Road, London WC1X 8HB
A CBS Company

Based on the television series Mike the Knight
© 2012 HIT (MTK) Limited/Nelvana Limited. A United Kingdom-Canada Co-production.

ISBN 978-0-85707-680-9
Printed and bound in China
10 9 8 7 6 5 4 3
www.simonandschuster.co.uk

MIKE THE KNIGHT

Meet Mike!

Mike is a knight,
so brave and so bold.
He's daring and strong,
but not very old.
Turn over the page
and join in our quest,
To learn why our hero
is simply the best!

I'm Mike the Knight.
Welcome to Glendragon!

My mission is to be a brave hero
just like my dad, the King. If you need
to find buried treasure, round up Vikings
or defend a castle, I'm at your service.

Knights always try to do
the right thing. If I get stuck,
I open my 'Big Book for
Little Knights-in-Training'.
It's packed full of handy hints!

Most days you'll find me in Glendragon Castle practising my knightly skills. When duty calls, I dash to my bedchamber. I can be dressed in my armour quicker than you can say 'Huzzah'!

Before I head out to save the day,
I reach for my sword and shield.
No knight should ever leave his
castle without them.

I never know where my
next mission will lead me,
but I'm not scared. Mike
the Knight is always
ready for adventure!

Galahad is my trusty steed – he's the finest
horse in the land! He can do silent sneaking,
tricky trotting and great galloping.

I make sure that Galahad stays in tip-top shape. He gets new shoes from Mr Blacksmith's stall. If he splashes in muddy puddles, I take him for a scrub-up at Hairy Harry's horse-wash!

My two brilliant best friends are both dragons!

Sparkie is enormous and breathes fire. As well as sharing my adventures, he's also the castle cook. When Sparkie serves up his famous Special Stew, we all ask for second helpings!

Squirt is a little dragon with a big heart. Even though he can't breathe fire, his water-squirting is sensational!

Sparkie, Squirt and I would do anything to help each other out. If one of us gets into trouble, the others always come to the rescue.

Sparkie, Squirt and Mike (that's me!)
We're as brave as three can be!

Sometimes I play with my little sister. Evie's a wizard-in-training, but she's still got heaps to learn! Her magic spells never seem to work out quite right. Once she even managed to shrink me, Sparkie and Squirt to mouse-size!

Oops!
Maybe there's a better spell...

Despite her magical mishaps,
Evie still manages to teach me
a thing or two. When we work
together, we make a first class
team. Sometimes our mum,
the Queen, is so impressed,
she gives us a royal favour!

My dad, the King of Glendragon, is busy exploring far-off lands, but he sends lots of postcards telling me all about his daring deeds. He's discovered new castles, rescued villages and battled mighty sea monsters!

With Dad away, it's up to me to protect the kingdom. My mum, Queen Martha, often asks me to lend a knightly hand.

Some jobs take
great courage
and strength…

**No magic,
Evie!**

…others aren't quite so exciting.

My missions have led me to the farthest corners of Glendragon! I've followed tricky trails into the Tall Tree Woods, combed beaches and climbed grassy mountains.

Mike the Knight isn't afraid of anything!

I've even
discovered
a crowd of
rowdy Vikings
and lived to
tell the tale.

Sometimes my missions have led me to new friends.
The first time I explored the Maze Caves
I met a family of trolls.

Now whenever I visit, Ma Troll bakes something special.
Pa Troll sings, dances and gives me friendly slaps on the back.

Ma and Pa Troll have a son, Trollee. Trollee wants to be a knight, just like me!

Trollee and I do all sorts of things together, from treasure hunts to knightly games.

If I'm not out on a bold new quest, you'll find me back at home. A castle is a brilliant place for knights-in-training to live! Glendragon has a banqueting hall for feasting, a throne room and a proper jousting arena.

Galahad and I spend lots of time training in the arena. We practise jousting with a lance and riding through obstacle courses. When I enter a tournament, the whole kingdom turns out to watch. If I try extra hard, I might win a trophy!

Faster, Galahad! Faster!

Not all of my missions go to plan, but I never, ever give up. It's the first rule of being a knight! When times are tough I know that Glendragon is full of friends to help me put things right again.

So what will my next adventure be? You'll have to wait and see. If someone needs help, you can count on me to come rushing to the rescue. By my sword, I'm Mike the Knight!

Be a knight, do it right!

More magical
Mike the Knight books
coming soon... HUZZAH!

MIKE and the Scary Dragons

MIKE Mike's Missions

www.miketheknight.com

www.simonandschuster.co.uk